Free Runner

by

James Lovegrove

First published in 2009 in Great Britain by
Barrington Stoke Ltd
18 Walker Street, Edinburgh, EH3 7LP

www.barringtonstoke.co.uk

ISBN: 978-1-84299-606-5

Printed in Great Britain by Bell & Bain Ltd

A Note from the Author

I first learned about Parkour, or Free Running, a few years ago. It was exciting and I was amazed. Then I saw clips of Free Runners in action on the BBC. I also watched two French films, one called *Taxi,* the other called *District 13.* Both of them had shots of Free Running.

I couldn't believe the skills these people had. They moved like acrobats. They were as nimble as cats. They seemed to have no fear of being killed or hurt.

I knew I wanted to write a story about Parkour. I also knew I wanted to write a story that was incredibly fast-paced, a flat-out sprint from start to finish. The two ideas seemed to fit together like a hand in a glove, and this book is the result.

A boy's father is in deadly danger. The clock stands at 23 minutes. The count-down has begun ...

This book is dedicated to Grace and Christopher Kunzler, in the hope that it might keep them quiet for a while!

Contents

Chapter 1
23 Minutes ...

"Here's the deal, Taj," said Rogan. He was looking out of the window of his flat. "You've got 23 minutes to make it all the way across the estate. Or your dad dies."

"No!" I yelled. "I can't. It's impossible. 23 minutes? Forget it."

"Mr Snuff has his orders," said Rogan. "At eight o'clock on the dot, just after your dad has shut up his shop, Snuff kills him. It's a fact. I can't stop it now."

"Yes, you can," I said. "Call Mr Snuff. Right now. Get on the phone and tell him the contract is off. It's cancelled. Whatever the word is."

Rogan shook his head.

"Sorry, kid," he said. He sounded as if he meant it. "I'd love to do that, really I would. But I can't. Mr Snuff never carries his mobile when he's on a job. He says he can't risk it. Think about it. What if he forgets to switch the phone off? He's waiting there, his target comes into sight, and all of a sudden *biddly-biddly-beep*, his mobile rings. Snuff's cover is blown. Target runs a mile. End of story."

"OK, let's call my dad, then," I said. "At his shop. Tell him to close up early. Lock the door, pull down the metal shutters, and go and hide in the back room."

"Not gonna happen," said Rogan. "Snuff is watching the shop right now from the subway round the corner. If he sees something dodgy

2

going on, he'll be in there like a shot. Plan A is to kill your dad as he's leaving. Take his cash. Make it look like a mugging gone wrong. But, if he has to, Snuff will go into the shop and kill him there. That's Plan B, his back-up plan. Mr Snuff always has a back-up plan and that's why he never fails. He always gets his man. It's something he's very proud of."

Rogan smiled then. Four of his top front teeth had been taken out and replaced with solid gold ones. Each gold tooth had a letter stamped onto it. Together the letters spelled out the word CASH. That was what Rogan loved most in all the world – money. He built his life around it. It was his own personal code. Money was his god.

Seeing Rogan smile, I wanted to smash his face in. This wasn't a joke, I thought. Nothing about this was in any way funny. It was my dad we were talking about. It was life or death for him. Rogan had sent a paid hit man to murder him in cold blood. How could he smile like that?

I didn't lose my temper. Hitting Rogan would not solve anything. Besides, he was way bigger than me, and knew quite a bit about fighting. Rogan would punch me back twice as hard as I punched him. If I was lucky, he'd only break my nose.

"So that's it, then," I said. "I have no choice. I've got to get across the estate in 23 minutes and warn my dad."

"Nope," said Rogan. "Yes, you do have to get across the estate, from Block B here to your dad's shop at Block X. But then you've got to find Mr Snuff and tell him I'm calling the hit off. Warning your dad won't do any good. You need to see Snuff."

"But the fastest I've ever done a run to Block X is 26 minutes."

"You know how good a Runner you are, Taj," Rogan said. "None of my other Runners come close, not even Diamond. You're the best. You're a legend. If anyone can make it in 23 minutes, you can."

Rogan looked at his watch. It was a chunky platinum Rolex, not a fake, the real thing. Five grand's worth of time-telling machine. A big fat piece of ticking bling.

"In fact," he said, "it's more like 22 minutes now. So you'd best get going."

I turned to go. I stopped at the door.

"What if Snuff doesn't believe me?" I said to Rogan. "What if he wants proof?"

"Good point. Hold on a mo."

Rogan rushed out of the room and vanished into the back rooms of his flat.

I waited.

Chapter 2
22 Minutes ...

I went on waiting. I was in a panic. I was frantic to get started. Every second I stayed in Rogan's flat was one less second I had to reach my dad. One second closer to my dad's death.

The flat was huge. Only Rogan had a flat this size. Everyone else on the estate had only three or four rooms. Rogan had at least twelve. He had a whole floor of a tower block to himself. He'd knocked four flats into one. No one else would have been allowed to do it. But then no one else could bribe the council planning department like Rogan could.

What Rogan wanted, Rogan got. He could get it by scaring people. But he liked to get it by paying them.

"Money's the way," he liked to say. "Money always gets things done. It's quick, clean and simple and it does the job. With money there are no come-backs and no draw-backs. Everyone's happy."

In other words: CASH.

The main room of the flat was larger than the whole of my own flat. It had windows at both ends. It had huge leather chairs. It had pictures on the walls – modern art. One of them was said to be a real Damien Hirst screen-print. I'd been told it was worth thousands of pounds. To me it looked like something I could have knocked up in ten minutes in the school art room.

The stereo was a top of the range Bose, linked to an iPod. The TV was a 40-inch plasma flatscreen Sony. It was hooked up to a games console, the latest PlayStation or Xbox, I didn't know which. Two kids slightly younger than me were playing *Halo* on it right now.

The kids were two of Rogan's Runners, same as I was. They were waiting here for Rogan to give them some work to do. There might be a package for them to take to someone on the estate, or they might have to go and pick up a package from somewhere on the estate. I knew this because that was my job too. I'd often waited here, like them, for Rogan to send me out on a run.

What was in the packages?

You didn't ask. You never asked. You just took them to or from wherever he told you, and when you came back you got paid.

These two Runners were beginners. Rogan was still training them. They'd get maybe £30 per run, £40 tops. They were still pretty slow. They didn't know all the tricks, the shortcuts, the moves. Not like me.

Me, I got £250 for a run. Rogan trusted me with his most important packages. These packages were the ones he really couldn't afford to get lost on the way, the ones he couldn't have falling into the hands of the police. I did a run for Rogan about twice a month. It was good money. I'd never had any reason to complain about how Rogan treated me. I'd even looked on him as my friend.

Until now.

The two new Runners had the sound turned off on the TV. Guns were blazing silently on the screen. They'd heard what Rogan and I had been saying. They knew just what was going on. And they weren't going to do a thing about it. Nothing to do with them. They kept their eyes fixed on the telly.

I didn't blame them. If it'd been me sitting there, I'd have done the same. Anyway, what *could* they do? They couldn't help. This was my problem and mine alone.

A minute passed. Then another. I was starting to think Rogan wasn't coming back. He'd gone off and forgotten about me. He didn't care. So my dad was going to die. So what? Wasn't *his* dad. Wasn't anyone *he* loved.

But then at last Rogan returned. He walked back into the main room with a mobile in his hand. It was a luxury slider phone. It had a camera, USB port, quad-band, and God knows how many other features. The shell was made of smoked glass, black and shiny.

Rogan slid it open and showed me the screen. He pressed a key with his finger. A small video clip opened and played.

The video clip showed Rogan himself, talking. He had just filmed it.

"Snuff," Rogan said on the phone screen. His face moved around a bit. It wasn't always in the centre of the screen. But the picture was crystal clear. At least five megapixels, I thought.

"Sanjeev Gosh is in the clear, OK?" the video clip went on. "Taj's dad is not going to shop me to the cops. Taj has shown me proof. So the hit is off. Is that clear? You'll still get your money, but the hit is off."

The clip ended there. Rogan had spoken the last four words of his message very loud and clear. *The hit is off*. There could be no mistake. Mr Snuff could not tell me he'd missed the point of the message, or not heard it right.

Rogan shut the phone. He dropped it into a brown padded envelope. He sealed the envelope and handed it to me.

"There," he said. "That's the best I can do."

I slipped the padded envelope inside the front of my hoodie and did up the zip.

"Thanks, Rogan," I said. "I hate your guts ... but thanks."

"I know. Now get going, Taj. It's 19 minutes to eight. Your dad's life depends on you. Go. Go!"

I went.

Chapter 3
19 Minutes ...

I didn't even think about taking the lift.
Too slow.

I went for the stairs.

Rogan's flat was on the sixth floor of Block
B. The stairs went downwards in a zigzag.
I jumped from one flight to the next. Each
time, I grabbed the metal hand-rail, vaulted it,
and landed on the set of steps below. Back and
forth, back and forth I went, with my knees
bent to soften the impact of each landing.
I reached the ground floor in less than 15
seconds.

I raced through the block's main entrance, out into the warm evening air. The sky was brown and orange. Street lights were starting to come on. At least, the ones no one had broken were.

There was an open space in front of the tower block. It was an area of tarmac with concrete bollards all round, which were there to stop people driving their cars onto it. The area was meant to be a kind of park, only without trees or grass or flowers. There were benches, a rusty climbing frame, and lots of black litter bins that hadn't been emptied for ages. Rubbish spilled out of the bins like the froth from an over-filled glass of beer. Most of the rubbish seemed to be McDonald's and KFC boxes, with scraps of food still in them. The local pigeons and rats were well fed on our estate.

I leapt from bench to black bin to concrete bollard. I didn't stop, didn't pause. Each precision jump led on to the next. I did a monkey-swing through the climbing frame. Some small kids were playing on it but they scattered when they saw me coming. Then I bounced off another bin, another bollard, and I'd crossed the open space and was on my way towards the next tower block.

So far it was easy. I wasn't panting yet. I wasn't even breathing hard. If this had been just any old run, I'd have been happy. I'd have been relaxed about how things were going.

But this wasn't just any old run.

It was the most important run I'd ever done. And I couldn't afford to slip up. One small stumble might mean the difference between my dad living and dying. If I fell and twisted my knee or hurt my ankle, that would be it. My dad would be dead.

I sprang onto a low wall and raced along the top of it. I kept my arms out for balance, like a tight-rope walker in a circus. At the end of the wall I just jumped off onto the ground.

On any other day I might have dived off and gone into a forward roll, tucking my head in and coming up on all fours. Not today, though. Today, every second counted. There was no time for any fancy stuff.

The next few hundred metres were just a dash across open ground. There was nothing to jump onto or off. There were no objects to give me more speed. It was just me and my two legs.

As I ran I was thinking of my dad.

My dad worked harder than anyone I knew. He opened his shop every morning at six and closed it at eight every evening. He did this even on weekends and bank holidays, and even when he was ill. The only day he took off each year was at Christmas.

My dad had always been like that, even before my mum died. His shop was the most important thing in his life. It was even more important to him, perhaps, than his wife and his only son.

"Work is what makes a man, Taj," my dad would say. "Without work a man is nothing. Nothing at all. He is just in the way, a waste of space. How can a man look after his family if he doesn't bring in money? How can he bear to look at himself in the mirror every morning if he is someone who, at the end of each day, has earned no money and got nothing done?"

My dad believed this even more after my mum died of breast cancer. It was weird. He could have worked a bit less hard, now that there was one less person to feed in the family. But no, he worked even harder. He got rid of his part-time assistant, Mrs Carling. He stopped taking lunch breaks. He always seemed to be at the shop. I hardly ever saw him at our flat. Our flat was just a place where my dad went when he needed to sleep. Gosh's General Store was his real home.

All this was so that my dad wouldn't have to think about Mum. As long as he was at the shop, keeping busy, he wouldn't have to deal with his grief over her death. He wouldn't have to think about all the time he should have spent with her, instead of working at the shop.

Of course, my dad didn't like me being one of Rogan's Runners. He should have been pleased. After all, I got a good wage off Rogan. I could buy stuff that none of the other kids at school could afford. He should have been proud of me for that reason.

But to my dad it wasn't a proper job.

"You are a slave to that Rogan," he often said to me. "You are his dog. He calls, you come. You fetch and carry for him, always wagging your tail. But he thinks no more of you than he would a pet."

My dad also knew that what Rogan was doing was pretty shady.

"You will get into trouble one of these days, Taj. Those packages you carry – one day, you'll get found out. You mark my words, boy."

But the package I was carrying right now would save my dad's life. Or so I hoped.

The next tower block loomed before me. It was Block E, and it was linked to several other blocks by a series of foot bridges. The foot bridges were on the third-storey level. They crossed roads, a canal, and a couple of areas of wasteland.

As I got closer to Block E, I groaned.

A police car was parked outside the block.

And there were two cops in the car, and they had spotted me and were getting out.

I knew these two.

PC Parks and WPC Kent.

Damn it!

Chapter 4

17 Minutes ...

I couldn't stop. I kept on running. I was hoping to dodge around the two cops.

But PC Parks lumbered towards me, blocking my way. This was easy for him to do. PC Parks was a right old porker. He was so fat, his double chin had a double chin.

I darted around him, but WPC Kent then came out of nowhere and grabbed me. Unlike her partner, WPC Kent was slim and fit. Her hand gripped my elbow like a steel trap.

"Whoa, whoa there, Taj," WPC Kent said. "Where are you off to in such a hurry?"

I wriggled, trying to slip out of her grasp.

"No time," I said. "Let me go!"

"Hold still," said PC Parks, grabbing my other arm. He was strong too, but in a fair fight between the two of them WPC Kent would take him down. The woman was as mean as she was lean.

I struggled even harder to get away.

PC Parks took his baton from his belt. He snapped it open to its full length.

"Don't make me use this on you, sonny," he said.

I went still. He meant what he said. PC Parks enjoyed whacking people with his baton, most of all people who were smaller than him and didn't have a weapon of their own. He was

21

a bully. He loved hurting people who couldn't fight back.

"We just want a word with you, Taj, that's all," said WPC Kent.

I looked her in the eye.

"Please," I begged. "Any other time. I'll talk to you as long as you want. Any other time. Just not now."

"What's so urgent you can't have a chat now?" said PC Parks. "What could be more important than helping out two of your friendly community police officers?"

"I – I can't explain," I said. "You'll just have to trust me."

There was no way I could tell them about Mr Snuff waiting to kill my dad. They might not believe me, and that in itself would be bad. But even worse, they might believe me. Then they'd get in their cop car and go racing round to my dad's shop. They'd have their lights flashing and their siren blaring. Mr Snuff would hear them coming, and he'd use Plan B instead of Plan A. He'd go into the shop, kill Dad, and be out of there before Parks and Kent arrived.

"This hasn't anything to do with your father, then?" said WPC Kent. She looked sly. "We've heard he's going to testify against your pal Rogan. Your dad's agreed to stand up in court and swear that Rogan has been up to all sorts of crimes. Drug dealing, bribery, paying for people to be beaten up, even murder ..."

"That's not true!" I shouted.

"So Rogan's done none of those things?" said PC Parks. He gave a snort. "Come on, Taj! Do you think we were born yesterday? Rogan's a criminal. You know that as well as we do. He's a crook and a gangster. Rotten to the core."

"Yes," I said. "No. I mean, it's not true that my dad's going to grass on Rogan."

"Oh?" said WPC Kent.

"It's just a rumour, what people are saying. A rumour that's got out of hand. Look, can I go now? You've 'had a word' with me, and I've got stuff I really need to do."

PC Parks looked at his partner. "What do you think, Kent?" he said. "It's coming up for eight o'clock. Maybe Taj is trying to get home in time to catch *EastEnders*. Maybe that's why he's in such a rush."

WPC Kent grinned at him. It wasn't a nice grin. Her black police waistcoat made her chest stick out like a hen's.

"I think the suspect is trying to fool us," she said. "I think we should take him back to the station and ask a few more questions. And I think we should search him when we get him to the station. We might well find something on him to prove he's been involved in some crime or other."

"Good idea," said PC Parks. "Maybe Taj's dad isn't willing to blab about Rogan, but Taj might be. And Taj will make a much better witness. He's one of Rogan's gang. We all know that. He's one of Rogan's Runners. With Taj's help, we could nail Rogan good and proper. And you know what that would mean for you and me, Kent. Promotion. No more hanging around a grotty estate in a police car, pretending we give a stuff about all the chavs and pikeys who live here. We'd be given nice, cosy desk jobs."

WPC Kent seemed to like this idea very much indeed.

Together, the two cops began to drag me towards their car.

"No!" I screamed, and kicked out at them.

PC Parks and WPC Kent were so shocked that they stood still. For a moment, just a moment, I felt both of them loosen their grip on me.

25

That was all the opening I needed. I yanked my arms free and was off like a bullet.

I headed for the front of Block E at full speed. The two cops came after me. WPC Kent was faster than her lardy partner. She was right behind me. I could almost feel her hand reaching for the back of my hoodie.

But then I launched myself into the air.

I was at a spot where two of Block E's outer walls met at right angles. I was inside the corner of the two walls, which meant I could kick off one of them with my right foot and the other with my left foot. I went up the face of the block like this, doing a "tic tac" all the way to the first floor. I heard WPC Kent swear below me. PC Parks threw his baton at me in frustrated fury. It rebounded off the wall just below my feet.

I perched on the edge of a first-floor balcony. Every flat on Block E had a small balcony outside it, with a metal railing round it. I stood up on the railing and grabbed the base of the balcony above. I pulled myself up with just my arms, a move known as a "muscle up". I did the same to get to the third floor.

An old man was standing on this balcony. He was using a watering can on some sunflowers which he had grown in pots. He was wearing a string vest and braces. A cigarette hung from his lips.

The old man stared at me. I stared at him.

The water poured from the can onto his shoes. The old man didn't even notice.

In spite of everything, I gave him a quick wink. Then I moved sideways on the railing to the next balcony along. I swung myself around the slab of wall between the two balconies. I kept going in this way, crab-walking along the side of the block. At last I reached a balcony that was next to one of the foot bridges. While I was doing this I heard the engine of a car start up. I knew it was the police car.

I dropped onto the wall of the foot bridge. From there I dropped onto the foot bridge itself. I was running as soon as I landed.

The police car revved and took off with a screech of tyres. I knew that PC Parks and WPC Kent would go on chasing me. They could tell something was up. They were keen to catch me.

It wasn't great news, but it could have been worse. I could run faster than them. I could get to places they couldn't hope to go in a car.

But they had delayed me.

And if I didn't reach my dad in time and it was the two cops who'd made me late, I swore I would find some way of making them pay.

Chapter 5

14 Minutes ...

The foot bridge went from Block E to Block F. From Block F, another foot bridge crossed over to Block G, with junctions that led off to Blocks H and I.

The police car raced along the roads below. Twice it passed directly under the foot bridge that I was on. I just ignored it. I focused on my running and nothing else.

People were walking along the foot bridges. I skirted around them if they didn't get out of my way. Sometimes I had to hop up onto the wall of the foot bridge and dart along that till I got past.

I did the same sort of thing when I was inside the tower blocks, running through to get to the next foot bridge. The public corridors in the blocks were narrow. There wasn't space to squeeze past anyone.

But the corridors often had overhead pipes. I swung on those, whizzing above the head of the person who was blocking me.

Or else I turned on my side and slid past the person. I did this to one old granny in Block H. She nearly had a heart attack. And as I was running onwards from her, she yelled after me. She looked like a sweet old dear but some of the language she came out with was pretty nasty. I'd have laughed, if I'd had the breath to spare.

To me, as I ran, the estate had become simply a set of objects to get across, over, under or around. I treated people much the same as a wall or a bollard, just another kind of obstacle. They moved, that was the only difference.

It was like solving a puzzle, at lightning speed. My body knew the moves. I hardly had to think about which of them to use. I tackled each problem as it came. I ducked or rolled or jumped or climbed. I did it almost by instinct.

Rogan had taught me this.

Rogan had spent some time in Paris a few years ago. There he'd learned Free Running, or *le Parkour* as it was called in France. Before that he had studied martial arts in China and Japan. Rogan enjoyed pushing his body to its limits and mastering new skills. He liked a challenge. That was one of the things I'd always admired about him.

I was 12 years old when I first saw Rogan practising *le Parkour*. He was at the skateboard park. He was leaping and spinning around among the ramps and half-pipes. I'd

31

never seen anything like it before. Rogan
looked as if he was dancing. Sometimes he
even looked as if he was flying. I was stunned
by it, and so were the skater boys. They were
standing there watching him too. Their
mouths were wide open and their boards hung
by their sides. They couldn't believe it. Rogan
was doing the sort of stunts they did, only
without a skateboard. It was just him and his
body, whirling here, there, everywhere. It was
graceful. It was beautiful. It was incredible.

I went up to Rogan afterwards and asked
him to show me how he did it. I knew who
Rogan was. I knew he was a bad guy and I
ought to steer clear of him. But I was 12, and I
was curious, and I was lonely. My mum had
died the year before. My dad drifted about like
a ghost. He was someone who haunted our
flat, not saying much when he was there, just
sort of passing through.

Rogan looked me up and down. Then he grinned. His four gold teeth glinted in the sunlight, a flash of CASH.

"All right, then," he said.

I was the first Runner he ever trained. We met week after week and Rogan passed on to me all the *Parkour* knowledge he had picked up in Paris. I soon became skilled at it. And it was because I was such a good pupil that Rogan got the idea of training more Runners. He'd always needed people to act as messengers, carrying his packages around the estate. Why not create a special group of Runners to do the job? With *Parkour* they could go anywhere. They could stay out of the clutches of the police. No one could catch them.

"*Parkour* is the art of escape," Rogan once told me. "In French the word means 'obstacle course', only they've spelled it a bit wrong. In English it would probably look like this."

He wrote down two words on a piece of paper: OBSTAKLE KOURSE.

"It's about getting from one place to another in the neatest possible way," Rogan went on. "It's about quick thinking, and energy flow, and total body control. And it's about avoiding things. Avoiding trouble most of all. That's why you're going to be so useful to me, Taj. You and all the other Runners I'll train. When you carry packages for me you'll use *Parkour* to stay out of trouble, and that means you'll be helping *me* stay out of trouble. Clever, eh?"

Only one other pupil of Rogan's came close to being as good a Runner as me. That was Diamond. She was tall and slim and she could run like a deer. At school she was the queen of the athletics track. She won every race she took part in, even if sometimes she had to cheat to do it. Once, Diamond tripped up another girl less than five metres from the finish line. Another time, she elbowed a rival in the face just as the starting pistol went. She was lucky not to have been spotted either time. But mostly she won the races fair and square. No one could keep up with her.

I had just got past Block H. I sneaked a glance at my watch. Not quite 11 minutes to eight. That was a nice surprise. I was making good progress and I had a serious shortcut planned. The shortcut would shave quite a bit of time off my journey. Maybe I *could* do this!

Then, who should I bump into, but Diamond.

Chapter 6
11 Minutes ...

'Bump' was the right word.

Diamond was out on an evening jog. She came bounding out of a side-alley. I saw her a moment too late. I couldn't stop. We collided. Hard. We both went down in a heap.

"Oof!"

"Yowch!"

We lay for several seconds, tangled together. I was dazed. Everything seemed a muddle. There was a hand in my face and I couldn't even tell if it was mine or Diamond's.

My head cleared.

"Gerroff!" I yelled.

I pushed Diamond off me and scrambled to my feet. Diamond got up too, shaking her head. Her hair beads rattled.

"What you doing, running into me like that, Taj?" she snapped.

"I didn't run into you. *You* ran into *me*," I told her. "Why don't you look where you're going?"

"Why don't *you*?" Diamond said. "You blind or just stupid?"

"Neither," I said. "And I'd love to stand here and swap insults, Diamond, but I can't. 'Bye!"

I set off. My knee was hurting a bit. I must have bruised it in the crash with Diamond. I'd also banged one of my elbows.

But the pain didn't matter. It would soon fade. Only my dad mattered.

I ran through a small parade of shops. It was much like the one where my dad had his shop. Most of the stores here had closed down, however. They had sheets of chipboard nailed over their windows. Graffiti tags and posters covered the chipboard.

As I came out of the parade of shops I glimpsed the police car. It was quite a way behind me now, still driving past Block G. I was nearly at Block K.

Blocks L, M and N stood in a row behind Block K. They were the largest three tower blocks on the estate. Behind them lay Blocks P and Q. Both of those blocks were derelict, nearly falling down. The residents had been moved out a few years ago. The council had then got in builders and cranes. They had promised that the two blocks would be made good as new. But it had never happened.

Scaffolding had been put up, and the cranes were still there, but building work hadn't yet begun and never would begin. Everyone knew the council didn't want to fix Blocks P and Q. It cost too much. The council was just waiting for them to collapse of their own accord, as they would do if left alone. That was the cheap way to solve the problem.

There were tall wire fences around Blocks P and Q. Signs on the fences warned "KEEP OUT" and "DANGER".

But I knew that going right through those two blocks would save me at least three minutes. Maybe even four.

So that was where I was making for.

As I got closer to Blocks P and Q, I heard footsteps behind me. It was someone running.

I looked over my shoulder.

Diamond.

She was sprinting after me to catch up. In no time she was running alongside me.

"So where you going?" Diamond asked.

"None of your business," I told her out of the side of my mouth. "Leave me alone."

"You trying to break your own record? Is that it?"

"Yeah, all right," I lied. "That's what I'm doing."

"I can help," she said. "Let me pace you."

"No. I told you, leave me alone."

Every word I spoke came out as a gasp. I was starting to feel short of breath. The non-stop speed of my run was beginning to wear me down. My chest ached and my legs were getting tired.

"Please, just go away!" I begged Diamond.

But Diamond wouldn't take no for an answer. She stuck beside me, her arms going like pistons.

"I'll keep pushing you," she said. "We'll do this together. Come on, it'll be great!"

I couldn't believe Diamond wanted to help me. That wasn't like her at all. But perhaps she did want me to break my own record, and I could guess why. If she stuck with me, she could see how I did it. She could learn my tricks and try to break the record herself some other time.

This was just what I needed! But how could I get rid of her? I couldn't. Diamond was as fast as me, and I was halfway through a run already, while she was fresh. There was no way I could put distance between her and me, not now. However much I speeded up, she could match me.

All I could do was try to ignore her. Rogan had taught me how important it was to focus

___

when running. To shut out distractions. To think only about the run itself.

Parkour was about being in the moment. You had to stay in your own head. You had to become your own little world. You should think of nothing outside you except the next obstacle, whatever it was.

There is no Diamond, I told myself. *I am on my own. She is not there.*

The fence around Blocks P and Q lay dead ahead. I raced towards it.

I heard Diamond groan. Her voice sounded far away, even though she was right beside me. I had blanked her out, but not altogether.

"Taj," she said, "you're not going to ...!"

I sprang at the fence. I went up it, slotting the toes of my trainers into the wire links. I vaulted over the top.

Follow me if you dare, Diamond, I thought.

42

I didn't expect she would.

But she did.

Chapter 7
9 Minutes ...

The scaffolding was like a giant steel web and I scuttled up through it like a human spider. Diamond kept close. She copied me, using almost all the same handholds and footholds that I did.

Five storeys up, I leapt off the scaffolding, into the empty block. My point of entry was a broken window. There were only a few pieces of broken glass left, sticking out from the frame. I hurled myself through in a Superman roll, not touching any of the glass. My body was arched. My arms were held forward. My hands hit the floor, and an instant later so did my head. I had my neck bent. My back came over. The rest of me followed. I did a somersault and sprang up on my toes.

Diamond was a split-second behind me. She Superman-rolled too.

But I was already off. I charged through the flat we had just entered. This had been someone's home, not so long ago. The wallpaper hung in shreds. A couple of stuffed toys had been left in a child's bedroom. They were wet and rotting. A shattered TV set lay on its side in the living room.

The main door hung at an angle off one hinge. I hurdled over it, at the same time swinging myself around with one hand on the frame.

"Taj!" Diamond called out behind me. "This is crazy! We're not supposed to be in here. We could get ourselves killed."

"Then *don't* be in here," I yelled back. "Turn around. Go home."

"Why are you risking your neck like this?"

"Because I don't have a choice," I said. "It's me or my dad."

I hadn't meant to say anything about my dad. The words just came out.

"Your dad?" said Diamond. We were scooting along a corridor now. The floor was littered with chunks of plaster and lumps of broken concrete. Our feet splashed through puddles of rainwater.

"Oh, don't tell me," Diamond went on. "Rogan. He's heard the rumour. About your dad."

"Only it's not true," I said. "The rumour's wrong. My dad isn't going to testify against him."

"How do you know that?"

"Look, why don't you just shut up?" I said. "Talking's slowing me down."

But Diamond wouldn't shut up.

"How do you know the rumour's not true?" she asked.

I decided to be honest with her. "I didn't know it," I said. "Not at first. When I first heard about what people were saying about my dad, I believed it. It seemed the sort of thing he would do, grass on Rogan to the police. My dad hates me working for Rogan. He's always on at me to give up. Maybe he thought this was the only way to stop me. If Rogan goes to prison, there'd be no more Rogan's Runners."

"But he must've known what might happen if Rogan found out," Diamond said. "Everyone on the estate knows what Rogan does. But no one's going to come forward and say so. No one's that stupid."

47

"My dad isn't stupid," I said. "But he's lost his wife. He feels like he's lost his son. Maybe he thinks he's got nothing left to lose. At least, that's what I *thought*."

A large pile of rubble lay in the way. I did a pop vault, kicking off the wall so that I shot up in the air instead of forwards.

"So I asked him," I went on, as I landed the other side of the rubble. "I asked my dad if what everyone was saying was true. He swore blind it wasn't. He said two detectives had come to the shop a week ago. They'd wanted to know if he'd talk to them about Rogan. They said they were investigating Rogan and they were closing in on him. They had almost enough evidence to arrest him. All they needed was someone on the estate to agree to be a witness against him. That was the one thing they didn't have and the one thing they couldn't do without. No witness, no case."

"And?" said Diamond.

"And my dad told me he refused," I said. "He wouldn't even talk to the detectives. He just clammed up, said nothing, and after a while the detectives saw they were getting nowhere and they went away."

"And you believed him?"

"Not altogether," I said. "So I sneaked into the shop one night while he was asleep. I know where my dad keeps the shop keys. I let myself in and I went into the back room and checked the CCTV tapes. Dad has a camera in the shop, filming everything. He has to, to catch shoplifters and in case someone tries to rob him. He turns it off at night. So I was safe. He wouldn't know I'd been in."

We crossed from Block P to Block Q along a walkway. Block Q was in much worse shape than P. Parts of it had collapsed. The floors had huge holes which Diamond and I had to leap over. Sometimes there was no floor at all and we were running along bare iron beams, the bones of the building.

One of the cranes was standing on the far side of this block. That was what I was aiming for. The crane rose up right next to Block Q, with its arm sticking out towards Block U.

"I found the tape for the day the detectives came and I checked it out," I said to Diamond. "My dad hadn't lied. He'd said almost nothing to them. Just 'Good afternoon' and 'How may I help you two gentlemen?'"

"So why did people think he'd grassed on them?" said Diamond.

"I don't know. I expect someone spotted the detectives coming out of the shop. Everyone knows that I'm a Rogan's Runner and that my dad doesn't like it. Someone got the idea my dad had invited the detectives to visit. They put two and two together and came up with five."

"And now everyone thinks your dad has it in for Rogan," Diamond said, "including Rogan himself."

"Bingo," I said. I leapt over yet another hole in the floor, my legs out at full stretch. Diamond followed.

"But Rogan doesn't know your dad is innocent?" she said.

"He does now. I showed him the CCTV tape. I only wish I'd done it sooner."

We'd reached the far edge of Block Q. There was scaffolding here, just as on Block P. I jumped from an open stairwell onto this framework of steel poles.

"So why the hurry to ...?" Diamond didn't finish the sentence. She'd worked it out. Rogan had put out a hit on my dad. I was trying to stop it happening.

Diamond's next words were "Taj, don't. No."

51

I was swinging from a horizontal piece of scaffolding, doing what was called an "underbar". I swung and swung, harder and harder, further and further back and forth. I was building up momentum. My legs were getting higher with each arc of my body.

It was a gap of at least four metres to the crane.

We were five storeys up.

"Taj!"

I let go of the scaffolding and flew out into space.

Chapter 8
6 Minutes ...

I thought I wasn't going to make it. For one awful, heart-stopping moment I was sure I was going to miss the crane and shoot right past it. I had got it wrong. I hadn't swung hard enough.

Falling five storeys to the ground – that would make quite a splat.

Then I slammed into the side of the crane. Somehow I managed to hook my arms around one of its struts. I clung on for several seconds, barely able to believe I was alive. I wanted to hang there for ever, just hugging that crane. I didn't want to let go. I loved that crane. It was the best crane in the world ever.

Then sense returned. I remembered my deadline. Less than six minutes to go.

I started to climb up the side of the crane. I had thought that five storeys would be high enough up but it wasn't. I still needed to get a little higher.

"Taj!" Diamond shouted from Block Q. "Taj, I'm not even going to think about following you *there*. You are truly mental, Taj. That was suicide. That was so stupid it's not even funny. That was, that was –"

She tried to think of the right word.

"That was *awesome*," she said at last, and she gave a whoop. "Totally awesome!"

I wanted to say thanks, and I wanted to tell Diamond that if she thought that was awesome, she hadn't seen anything yet. But I was too busy with other things. Like not getting careless and falling off the crane. So I just kept on climbing.

It wasn't long before I reached the control cab, just below the crane's arm. I levered myself up around the control cab and onto the arm. Moments later I was standing on top of it.

I took a long, deep breath. I needed to steady myself now. Every footstep counted here. One slip, and that would be that.

The arm of the crane stretched out before me, narrowing to a point. It was shaped like a triangle and I was on the tip of it, perched on a long thin steel girder no more than 50 centimetres wide.

Block U stood beyond the tip of the arm. Gosh's General Store lay on the other side of that block. The parade of shops that included my dad's ran between Blocks U and X at ground level.

I heard a thin, wailing sound some way off. The police car siren. PC Parks and WPC Kent most likely didn't know where I was any more. But they weren't giving up, were they?

I shrugged.

It was hard to judge the gap from the end of the crane arm to the side of Block U. I guessed it was perhaps nine metres, or even ten.

A sloping glass roof stuck out from the side of the block, level with the fourth floor. The roof covered half of a large outdoor terrace. It was almost just below the crane arm.

I blinked hard. Sweat trickled into my eyes. I wiped my brow with my sleeve.

I tensed, getting ready to move.

Suddenly I heard Rogan's voice in my head.

"Flow, Taj," his voice said. "Above all, *Parkour* is about flow."

These were words from one of our training sessions together. Rogan would often say them. He'd repeat them over and over like the chorus of a song, till they were worn into my mind and I could recall them exactly, as now.

"It's about each movement leading smoothly on to the next," Rogan's voice said. "So smoothly you can't tell where one ends and the other begins. You don't think. You don't even feel. You just *flow*."

Just then I loathed Rogan more than I'd ever loathed anyone. I would never forgive him for trying to have my dad killed. I understood that Rogan was the sort of man who would protect himself at any price. But it showed how little he respected me. I'd thought he was my friend as well as someone I worked for. I'd thought we shared a bond. How wrong could you get?

This was the last run I would ever do. I was certain of that. Rogan and I were finished.

_____

Still, I would always be grateful to Rogan for everything he had taught me.

Flow.

The jump from Block Q to the crane had been near-suicide.

The move I was planning to do next wasn't even near-suicide.

It was almost certain death.

Flow.

But oddly enough I felt no fear. I had never felt more calm, in fact.

Either I succeeded or I failed. Either I lived or I died. Either I got to Mr Snuff before he got to my dad, or I didn't. It was everything or nothing, and I could hardly tell the difference between the two.

The world was that simple to me now.

And because it was so simple, I felt a weird, wonderful sense of freedom.

Flow.

I began to run along the top of the crane arm, placing one foot in front of the other. I barely thought about what I was doing. If I had thought about it, I expect I would have stopped dead in my tracks. All I knew was that I had to gather as much speed as I could. I needed to be sprinting by the time I reached the end of the crane arm.

The end arrived soon – sooner than I'd expected. Suddenly there was no more crane arm left. I kicked off, throwing myself out into space. Had I been going fast enough? My arms spun like windmills. For a time I felt as if I was flying.

Then the glass roof was below me. It rose up towards me with alarming speed. I bent my knees and braced myself for the impact.

Chapter 9
5 Minutes ...

Crunch!

That was the sound of glass breaking as my feet hit it.

But it was shatter-proof glass. A network of tiny wires ran through the panes. The glass cracked but did not break. The wires held it together.

Crunch!

That was the sound of me rebounding then hitting the roof again, further down. This time it was not my feet but my shoulder that landed first.

Crunch!

I bounced off again and banged back onto the glass a third time.

I'd turned over and landed on my bum. Next thing I knew, I was shooting down the roof in a sitting position. It was like being on one of those huge slides at a theme park. I slipped down the slope, until all at once the roof ended. Then I was falling onto the terrace below.

Without thinking, I bent my knees again. I came down on my toes, and rolled.

I rolled several times, and ended up on my front. My legs and arms were sprawled out. My face was pressed flat against the concrete floor of the terrace.

It wasn't a perfect landing by any means. I'd been going too fast for that. It was, in fact, a pretty clumsy landing. But really, I couldn't complain.

My shoulder hurt. My bum hurt. I'd grazed my cheek.

But I was alive. I was in one piece. I got slowly to my feet and checked myself over. No bones were broken. I felt a bit dizzy but everything seemed, on the whole, to be in working order.

I looked up. There were white marks on the roof, three of them in a row, one for each time I'd hit the glass. Each mark was a pattern of cracks, like a snowflake. Each was smaller than the one above.

I felt a mixture of astonishment and relief. A leap like the one I'd just done was a one-in-a-million shot. And I'd pulled it off. I was still alive.

But I would have to wait to tell myself what a hero I'd been. My watch said it was nearly five to eight. I prayed my watch was fast. I prayed my dad would be a bit late in closing the shop tonight. As I started to make my way down through Block U, I prayed for a lot of things.

Chapter 10
3 Minutes ...

Rogan had said that Mr Snuff was waiting in the subway just around the corner from the shop. I knew the exact spot where he would be. You could see the shop from the subway entrance. Mr Snuff would be standing just inside the entrance, in the shadows. He'd be hiding in there, silent and still, just one more shadow.

Leaving the shop at eight o'clock on the dot, my dad would then walk to the subway. It went beneath a main road and led to Block Y, where our flat was.

None of the lights worked in the subway. The bulbs had frazzled out one by one and the council couldn't be bothered to put in new ones. On dark nights it was pitch black in there. In winter, my dad always carried a torch to light his way home.

In my mind I could see Mr Snuff watching as my dad strolled closer. I could see him pull out his knife. The blade would shine in the dark of the subway.

Mr Snuff was like a phantom. A lot of people on the estate were sure he didn't even exist. They thought he was a story made up by Rogan. They thought Rogan had invented Mr Snuff in order to scare everyone. I'd heard small children talking about Mr Snuff as if he was some kind of bogey-man. He could walk through walls, they said. He could hide under your bed and you'd never know he was there ... until he slit your throat with his knife and left you choking on your own blood.

None of this was true. Mr Snuff was just a man. I'd met him a few times at Rogan's place. Mr Snuff was pale and thin, with white hair that he shaved close to his scalp. It looked like a coating of frost on his head.

Mr Snuff never said much. He kept to himself. I'd see him sitting in the corner of the main room, sipping a Coke or rolling himself a cigarette. He didn't talk. He didn't smile much either. But when he did, he showed teeth that were so yellow, they looked like two rows of sweetcorn.

If Rogan needed to threaten someone, he sent Mr Snuff. If he needed someone beaten up, he sent Mr Snuff. Mr Snuff was Rogan's fist, so to speak. He was like a punch that Rogan could land anywhere, any time, on anyone who tried to mess with him.

I came down through Block U, thinking about Mr Snuff in the subway. I leapt from the second storey of the block onto the top of a lamp post. From there I did a hanging drop onto a parked car. The car had been dumped, and some vandals had come along and attacked it, stripped it bare. Now the car was just a shell, without tyres or windows. So it didn't matter that I put one more dent in the roof by dropping onto it.

The car was sitting outside the community centre. This was a single-storey prefab building that had been gutted by fire last year. The council, of course, were still trying to decide whether to replace it. They'd go on debating forever.

I sprang from the car to the roof of the community centre. I scrambled across the roof on all fours, doing a "cat balance". At the far end, I paused.

From here I had clear view of the subway entrance. I could also see the parade of shops. There was no one about. The parade was deserted. But the lights were on in the window of Gosh's General Store. My dad must still be there.

For the first time since leaving Rogan's flat, I was able to feel hope. I felt a sense of triumph as well. I'd done the impossible. I'd got there in time. I hadn't just broken my own record, I'd *smashed* it.

I glimpsed a movement in the subway shadows. I saw a pale arm bending upwards. It was a faint outline, more a blur than anything definite. It was there, then gone in an instant.

It was Mr Snuff, looking at his watch.

If his watch told the same time as me, there was now just under three minutes to go.

I got ready to vault down from the community centre roof. I reached inside my hoodie for the padded envelope with Rogan's phone in it.

It wasn't there.

The padded envelope was gone.

I undid the zip of my hoodie. I checked inside my T-shirt. I checked the waistband of my trackie bottoms. I patted myself all over. I tried to hold down the panic that was rising in me.

The envelope just wasn't there.

I must have dropped it. Somewhere on the way over here the envelope had slipped out of my hoodie. I hadn't even noticed.

I'd lost the phone and the video clip message that would save my dad's life.

After all I'd been through, I'd failed.

A little over two minutes left, and my dad was as good as dead.

Chapter 11

2 Minutes ...

I was gutted. I wanted to scream. I wanted to cry with anger and despair.

But I couldn't do that.

There was only one thing for it.

I came down off the roof and headed for the subway. I might not have Rogan's message any more, but I could still talk to Mr Snuff. Maybe I could make him believe me. Maybe he might not carry out the hit.

Yeah, right.

It was worth a try, anyway. And it was better than doing nothing.

The subway entrance was a square of blackness that just got bigger, and blacker, as I came nearer. I didn't make any effort to hide myself. I wanted Mr Snuff to see me coming.

I could feel his gaze on me. I could feel him watching me from the darkness. I stared at the place where I knew he was standing. I needed him to know that I knew he was there.

Finally I stopped, just a few metres from the subway entrance.

"Mr Snuff?" I said.

My mouth was so dry that it felt as if I'd gulped down a handful of dust.

"Mr Snuff?" I said again. The words came back at me like an echo from the subway, sounding dull and hollow.

71

It struck me that Mr Snuff might not be there at all. Perhaps he had chosen to hide somewhere else and I'd only thought I'd seen that arm moving. If so, then I was speaking into empty space, and the only thing I would ever hear back from the subway was the sound of my own voice.

Then a reply came.

"What?"

Mr Snuff spoke in a raspy whisper, like a saw being pulled through wood.

"What do you want, Taj?" he said.

"You know what I want," I told him. I'd started to tremble. I couldn't help it. "It can only be one thing. You're going to kill my dad. I'm begging you, please, don't."

There was silence from the subway.

Then Mr Snuff said, "Did Rogan send you?"

"Yes," I said. It wasn't quite true but it wasn't a lie either. "He said to tell you the hit is off. My dad isn't going to testify against him. He never was."

There was more silence.

"Nice try, Taj," Mr Snuff said at last. "But it's no good. I've got no reason to believe you, do I? You can't just turn up and expect me to take your word for it that Rogan says the hit is off. That's not how it works. I need proof."

"I don't have proof," I said, in despair.

"Then sorry. It's tough luck, but there it is. Your dad's done for. And don't try to stop me, Taj," Mr Snuff added. "Don't get in my way. Don't even think about it. It won't be good for you and it won't change the result either. You'll die and so will your dad. So step aside – right now – and let me get on with it. Or else."

I looked over my shoulder. The lights had gone off in the shop. The shutters had come down in front of the window. They were worked by a switch inside the shop. And now here was my dad, stepping out of the door. He turned, keys in hand, and started locking up.

He looked small and old to me then. His shoulders were hunched. His arms were skinny. I could see the small brown circle of his bald spot as he bent down to attach a padlock to the bottom of the shutters.

My dad had no idea he had less than a minute to live. Mixed feelings of pity and fear and love filled my mind.

I had to warn him. I had to give him a chance to escape, even if it cost me my own life.

All of a sudden Mr Snuff was standing right beside me. I hadn't heard him. He'd moved without making a sound.

His hand clamped tight over my mouth. I could just see the blade of a knife hovering at my neck.

"Not one word," Mr Snuff hissed. "Or I cut you open. Not one word. Got that?"

I nodded numbly.

Mr Snuff drew me back into the shadows of the subway. He pushed me against the wall, his hand still pressed to my face. He held me there while my dad left the shop and strolled towards us.

My dad was humming softly to himself. To him this was just a normal evening, the end of another day's hard work. His keys jangled in his hand.

This was it.

Only a few seconds left.

I was out of time.

Chapter 12

Out of Time

The shout startled me. It startled my dad. It even startled Mr Snuff.

"Wait! Hold on!"

Someone was running towards us from the parade of shops.

It was Diamond, and she had something in her hand. She was running fast, and I couldn't quite make out what she was holding. But it was brown, square and flattish, and looked very much like a padded envelope.

"Wait!" Diamond called out again.

My dad stopped and turned. Mr Snuff let out a soft grunt. He was annoyed.

"Mr Gosh," said Diamond.

"Yes?" said my dad. "Do I know you? Oh, wait, I've seen you around. You're a Runner, aren't you? You work for that man."

My dad didn't like to say Rogan's name if he didn't have to. But the way he spat out "that man" left no doubt who he was talking about.

Diamond skidded to a halt beside him, panting hard. "I'm Diamond," she said. "And I need to find your son. Where is he? Where's Taj?"

My dad gave a shrug and a sigh. "He should be at home doing his homework," he said. "But I suspect he isn't. I expect he's out running around, as usual. Can I help?"

Diamond bent over, one hand on one knee, getting her wind back. I could see now that it

77

was a padded envelope in her other hand. Could it even be ... *my* padded envelope?

I felt something flicker within my chest, like a tiny flame of hope sparking into life.

"This belongs to Taj," Diamond said to my dad, holding up the envelope. "It must've fallen out of his hoodie. We were running together but he lost me in Block ..." She was about to say Block Q, but stopped herself. "I don't remember which block. I found the envelope on the floor as I was going back the way we came. I wouldn't have known it was his, except I looked inside."

"And what is inside?" said my dad, in a scornful voice. "Drugs? Dirty money? A gun? What?"

Diamond pulled out Rogan's phone.

"Ah," said my dad. "No, I don't think that *is* Taj's. His phone is red, not black."

"No, wait," said Diamond. She slid the phone open. "Only one person on the estate could own a phone like this. But I thought I'd check the memory anyway, just to be sure. And I found this."

She pressed the keypad.

Rogan's video clip started to play.

"Snuff. Sanjeev Gosh is in the clear, OK? Taj's dad is not going to shop me to the cops."

The message sounded tinny and very faint. Mr Snuff and I could only just hear it.

But we *could* hear it, that was the main thing. We could hear every word.

"You'll still get your money," Rogan said on the video clip, "but the hit is off."

My dad stared at the phone, and then at Diamond.

Meanwhile Mr Snuff stared at me, his eyes just centimetres from mine.

"Oh," said my dad. "Play that again."

Diamond did as he asked.

Mr Snuff listened. His hand remained over my mouth, pressing hard.

"That's real, isn't it?" my dad said to Diamond. "It isn't a joke."

Mr Snuff's eyes seemed to be saying the same thing to me.

I nodded to Mr Snuff, telling him yes, it was real. It was the proof he had asked for a short while ago, the proof I hadn't been able to give him then.

Mr Snuff let go of me. He put his finger to his lips.

"Shhh," he said.

And then, just like that, he was gone. He sank back into the blackness of the subway, like ice melting into ink.

I didn't move for several heart-beats. I couldn't. I was glued to the spot.

When at last I got control of my legs again, I stumbled out of the subway.

"Dad!" I called out. "Diamond!"

I fell into my dad's arms and hugged him. He hugged me back. His hug wasn't very tight at first, but then it got tighter and tighter.

"I don't quite know what's going on," my dad said. "And I don't think I *want* to know. But I do believe I should say thanks to you, Taj. Shouldn't I?"

"Thanks will do fine, Dad," I said.

We broke apart. I turned to Diamond.

"Oh, what the hell," I said, and hugged her too.

She was sweaty but still smelled nice. Her body was firm and warm. I liked the way her hair beads tickled against my neck.

"It was good of you to do that," I told her. "Bring the phone here. I know you didn't have to."

"Yes, I did," Diamond replied. "I just had to after that stunt with the crane. *Both* those stunts. Respect, Taj. You're the best Runner, that's for sure."

"Not any more," I said. "I've decided I'm retired. You're the best Runner now."

Diamond looked puzzled. And then she looked pleased.

"Hang on," said my dad. "What stunt is this? What crane? What's Diamond talking about? Taj ..."

Before I could think of what to tell him, a police siren blared. A police car pulled up alongside the three of us. Out stepped PC Parks and WPC Kent.

"Ah, got you now!" declared PC Parks, hurrying towards us, puffing hard. "Taj Gosh, I'm placing you under arrest. What are the charges, Kent?"

"Resisting arrest," said WPC Kent. "Assault on a police officer."

"What?" said my dad. He stepped between me and the two cops. His stuck his hands on his hips. "What are you talking about, Constable Parks? Taj hasn't done any of those things. I'm sure he hasn't. This is nonsense! My son is a hero. He just saved my life."

PC Parks brandished a set of handcuffs.

"With all due respect, Mr Gosh," he said, "your son isn't a hero. He's a walking ASBO, and we're taking him in."

"Taj isn't perfect, I admit," said my dad. "But assault? I don't think so."

While this was going on, I looked at Diamond. She looked at me.

"Are you sure about being retired?" Diamond whispered.

I frowned at her, then saw what she was getting at.

"Well, maybe not *retired* retired," I said. "I've still got one last run left in me."

She grinned at me. I grinned back.

"Hey!" shouted PC Parks. "Hey! You two, stop! Come back here!"

But Diamond and I were already off at a dash. PC Parks lumbered off after us like an elephant in uniform. WPC Kent gave chase too.

Neither of them stood a chance. In no time Diamond and I were up the side of Block U and scampering from balcony to window ledge.

I took a look back at my dad, shortly before he was lost from sight.

He was gazing up at me, and his face was split by a huge, proud smile.

Barrington Stoke would like to thank all its readers for commenting on the manuscript before publication and in particular:

Kieran Lee Ball
Aaran Shane Bird
Olivia Boyd
Mark Bradley
Samantha Brain
S. W. Burns
Julie Carss
Matthew Claffey
Antony Cree
Dean Gallagher
Rema Gifford
Kameron Hammet
Lorna Henderson

Tammy Nicholls
Ashleigh O'Brien
Katherine Ofsarnie
F. Poxton
Sam Price
Jack Redman
Sarah Rhodes
Shannen Sidebottom
Jodie Stringer
Leanne Turner
Harry Wall
Harley Walters
Nicole Wild

Become a Consultant!

Would you like to give us feedback on our titles before they are published? Contact us at the email address below – we'd love to hear from you!

info@barringtonstoke.co.uk
www.barringtonstoke.co.uk

Great reads – no problem!

Barrington Stoke books are:

Great stories – from thrillers to comedy to horror, and all by the best writers around!

No hassle – fast reads with no boring bits, and a story that doesn't let go of you till the last page.

Short – the perfect size for a fast, fun read.

We use our own font and paper to make it easier to read our books. And we ask teenagers like you, who want a no-hassle read, to check every book before it's published.

That way, we know for sure that every Barrington Stoke book is a great read for everyone.

Check out www.barringtonstoke.co.uk for more info about Barrington Stoke and our books!

Kill Swap

A boy with a *big* problem.
A man who says he has
the answer.
Darkness.
A gun.
Someone's about to die.

The nightmare has just
become real.

Cold Keep

The sun sets on the icy
wastelands of Cold Keep,
and Yana faces the
greatest danger of her life.
The Shadow Trolls are
hunting. And Yana must
fight them alone.

She will come back a hero
— if she comes back at all.

The House of Lazarus

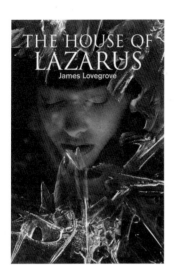

In the House of Lazarus, they say they can keep people alive forever. It costs a lot for Joey to keep his mum there and he finds it hard to pay the rent, but he knows his mum didn't want to die. Then Joey has a dream that makes him wonder if he has done the right thing ...

Ant God

Big Ideas. Big and weird Ideas. That's what Dan's best friend Jason does best. Like when he decided cats ruled the world. Now he's made the Truth Glasses. He says they show him things ... things that shouldn't be seen. Dan's got a bad feeling that Jason's gone one step too far this time ...

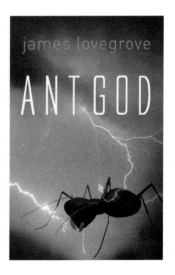

You can order these books directly from our website at
www.barringtonstoke.co.uk